P9-CQJ-764

This book belongs to...

Chloe Karynah

I got this book at the
WES Family Reading Night Book Swap!

This book belongs to:
Name: _____

*Dr. Seuss's real name was Theodor Geisel. On books he wrote to be illustrated by others, he used the name LeSieg, which is Geisel spelled backward.

Originally published in a different form by Random House, Inc., New York, and in Canada by Random House of Canada Limited, Toronto ISBN 978-0-679-89247-2 (board) — ISBN 978-0-394-90019-3 (lib. bdg.).

BEGINNER BOOKS and colophon and RANDOM HOUSE and colophon are registered trademarks of Random House, Inc.

SCHOLASTIC and associated logos are trademarks and/or registered trademarks of Scholastic Inc.

This BOOK CLUB EDITION published by Scholastic Inc.
90 Old Sherman Turnpike, Danbury, Connecticut 06816.

ISBN 9-999-09882-7

Printed in the U.S.A.

First Scholastic printing, March 2007

Ten Apples Up On Top!

By
Dr. Seuss*

*Writing as
Theo. LeSieg

Illustrated by
Roy McKie

BEGINNER BOOKS
A Division of Random House, Inc.

SCHOLASTIC INC.
New York   Toronto   London   Auckland   Sydney
Mexico City   New Delhi   Hong Kong   Buenos Aires

One apple
up on top!

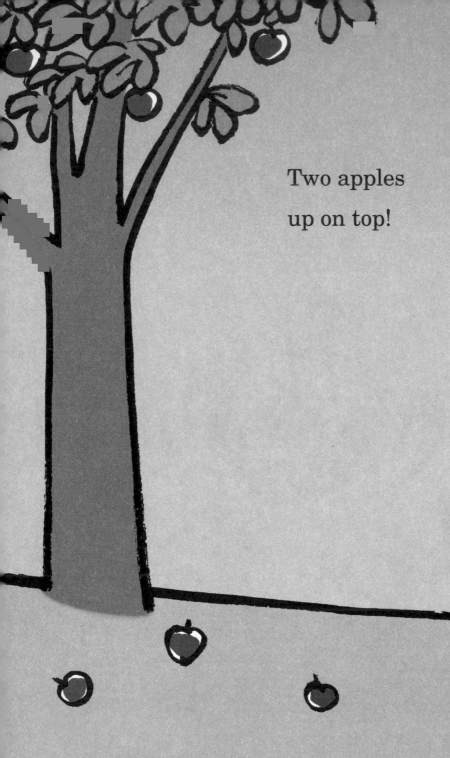

Two apples

up on top!

Look, you.

I can do it, too!

Look!

See!

I can do three!

Three . . .

Three . . .

I see.

I see.

You can do three
but I can do more.
You have three
but I have four.

Look! See, now.

I can hop

with four apples

up on top.

And I can hop

up on a tree

with four apples

up on me.

Look here, you two.

See here, you two.

I can get five

on top.

Can you?

I am so good

I will not stop.

Five!

Now six!

Now seven on top!

Seven apples

up on top!

Five, six, seven!

Fun, fun, fun!

Seven, six, five,

four, three, two, one!

I am

so good

they will not dro

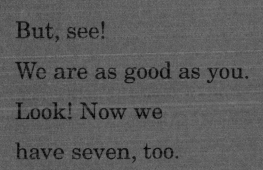

But, see!

We are as good as you.

Look! Now we

have seven, too.

And now, see here.

Eight! Eight on top!

Eight apples up!

Not one will drop.

Eight! Eight!
And we can skate.
Look now!
We can skate
with eight.

But I can do nine.
And hop!
And drink!
You can not do this,
I think.

We can! We can!

We can do it, too.

See here.

We are as good as you!

We all are very good,
I think.
With nine, we all
can hop and drink.

Nine is very good.
But then . . .
Come on and we
will make it ten!

Look!

Ten

apples

up

on

top!

We are not

going to let them drop!

Look out!
Look out!
I see a mop.

I will make

the apples fall.

Get out. Get out. You!

One and all!

Come on! Come on!
Come down this hall.
We must not let
our apples fall!

Out of our way!

We can not stop.

We can not let

our apples drop.

This is not good.
What will we do?
They want to get
our apples, too.

They will get them
if we let them.
Come! We can not
let them get them.

Look out!

The mop!

The mop!

The mop!

You can not stop
our apple fun.
Our apples will not drop.
Not one!

Come on! Come on!
Come one! Come all!
We have to make
the apples fall.

They must not get
our apples down.
Come on! Come on!
Get out of town!

Apples!

Apples up on top!

All of this

must stop

STOP

STOP!

Now all our fun
is going to stop!
Our apples all
are going to drop.

Look!
Ten apples
on us all!

What fun!
We will not
let them fall.